D1548596

THE ZOMBIE
OF GREAT PERU

OR

THE COUNTESS OF
COCAGNE

zase

LE
ZOMBI
DU GRAND
PEROU
OU
LA COMTESSE
DE
COCAGNE.

le marquis de quinexe

Nouvelement imprimé le qu....
Février 1697.

THE ZOMBIE
OF GREAT PERU
OR
THE COUNTESS OF COCAGNE

Pierre-Corneille Blessebois

WITH A PREFACE BY
GUILLAUME
APOLLINAIRE

Translated from the French by

Doug Skinner

BLACK SCAT BOOKS
2015

THE ZOMBIE OF GREAT PERU

Le zombi du Grand Pérou, ou la Comtesse de Cocagne
by Pierre-Corneille Blessebois

Translated from the French by Doug Skinner

ISBN-13 978-0-692-40974-9

First Edition

*Cover art & book design
by Norman Conquest*

Black Scat Books
E-mail: **blackscat@outlook.com**
Web: **BlackScatBooks.com**

BLESSEBOIS AND THE ZOMBIE

by Doug Skinner

Le Zombi du Grand Pérou, ou la Comtesse de Cocagne is a curious little book. It was published with no indication of author or place, but with a specific date: November 15, 1697. It's a small volume of 155 pages, containing a "historiette" in prose and verse, followed by a *"Portrait de la Comtesse de Cocagne"* in verse. It's rare; three or four copies are known.

It was only in 1829 that the bibliophile Charles Nodier identified the author as Pierre-Corneille Blessebois, based on internal evidence (the narrator calls himself a "crow," a *corneille*, in two of the verses) and on the similarity of some of the verses to others published under that name. Blessebois remained a mysterious figure for many years. Some bibliographers suspected that he was fictional, perhaps a pseudonym for another writer.

It was also suggested that there were two Blessebois, as the name appeared on both religious and pornographic works. *Le Zombi* was reprinted in 1860 in Brussels, by A. Lacroix, with a preface by Marc de Montifaud (a pseudonym for Madame Quivogne de Montifaud). Another edition appeared in Paris in 1862, with a preface by Édouard Cléder. Both added information about the elusive author, and about the setting: Grand Pérou was a sugar plantation in Guadeloupe. Mme. de Montifaud championed Blessebois, calling him "one of the most persecuted literary men of his time... always suspect to the church and state"; she earned eight days of prison in 1867 for publishing more of his works.

Pierre Louÿs, besides writing some fairly smutty stuff himself, had a scholarly interest in erotica. Around 1916, he became curious about Blessebois, and about *Le Zombi* in particular. Unfortunately, his friend Louis Loviot found his enthusiasm contagious, and published his own research before Louÿs, enraging Louÿs. Building on both of their work, Frédéric

Lachèvre published a biography in 1927, calling Blessebois the "Casanova of the 17th century." This seems unfair to Casanova, who was a model of propriety in comparison.

Blessebois, it turns out, did exist. His real name was Paul-Alexis Blessebois, and he was born sometime around 1646, in Verneuil-sur-Avre, the seventh of eight children. His father, Paul Blessebois, was a tax collector, his mother was Madeleine (or Julienne) Gaultier. Although little is known of his childhood, we do know that his father died when he was eleven, and that he soon renounced his family's Protestantism. He also changed his name to Pierre-Corneille, presumably in imitation of the playwright. It later turns up in various combi-

nations: Pierre-Corneille Blessebois, Pierre-Corneille de Blessebois,
Pierre de Corneille Blessebois, and
Pierre-Blessebois Corneille, among
others. By his early twenties, he
had become so industrious a wom-
anizer that he had to flee to Alençon, his father's hometown (he later
claimed that forty women vied for
his favors in one half year). He continued to make trouble, however,
publishing his first book, *Aventures
du Parc d'Alençon*, boasting of his
conquests and ridiculing his rivals.

Meanwhile, a local functionary,
Bernard Hector de Marle, had been
revising the tax records, and ended
the Blessebois family's exemption
(under the curious code, bourgeois,
clergy and nobility were untaxed).
In response, Blessebois and his

brother Philippe returned to Verneuil in 1670 and burned down the family home, to destroy the tax records. Philippe disappeared, but Pierre-Corneille was sentenced to banishment, a 500 pound fine, and confiscation of all his goods. Since he didn't have 500 pounds, he was put in prison, where he entertained his mistresses and wrote insulting acrostics about de Marle.

In 1671, his mother died, and he was released, with orders to leave the country. Instead, he ran off with one of the aforesaid mistresses, Marthe de Hayer (or de Sçay). After signing a marriage contract and pocketing a dowry of 2580 pounds, he then left for Holland to join the army. On his way, he told Marthe to wait for him, and lodged her in a brothel.

When he returned to Paris the next year, Marthe was waiting for him with a breach of promise suit. He explained to the court that he couldn't marry her, pointing to her stay in the brothel as proof that she was a prostitute. This earned him another prison sentence. He tried to marry her off to the brother of another prisoner, and solaced himself by himself writing invective against her, as well as a life of Jesus. Here's a sample of the former:

"Your eyes are more hollow and less brilliant than nutshells; your nose is a retreat which nature has stuffed with so much filth that nobody can approach you without suffocating; and your mouth is filled with more worms than rotten cheese..."

Despite his orders of banishment, he turned up in Normandy in 1674, where he killed a certain M. de Verdin, the husband of another of his girlfriends. He celebrated the occasion with a poem boasting about how much money she had given him, and how much she enjoyed sex with him. He then fled to Holland, where he wrote more polemics against Marthe, and tried to make money as both sailor and gigolo. He was back in France in 1676, and was back in prison after a couple of years, this time for beating a woman and her daughter. He tried to bargain for release by claiming knowledge about the scandal then surrounding Louis XIV's mistress, Mme de Montespan, and her involvement with the sorcerer La Voisin. He was unsuccessful.

On release, he was convicted of desertion from the navy, and, in 1681, condemned to life as a galley slave. After three years, he was declared an invalid, and shipped off as a conscript to Guadeloupe, banned from "entering France again under any pretext whatsoever." There he was sold to Marguerite la Garrigue, widow of Jean Dupont, owner of a large sugar plantation in Basse-Terre.

After, perhaps, the ill-advised antics described in *Le Zombi* (although we have every reason to suspect his word), Blessebois ended up in prison, where he was sentenced to make a public apology in church in 1690. It's not known if he died in Guadeloupe, or managed to sneak back into France. *Le Zombi* appeared in 1697: some scholars argue that it was published in Rouen; others that it was published in the Antilles, which would make it one of the first examples of colonial literature.

The story of *Le Zombi* is simple. A beautiful Creole, the Countess of Cocagne, has quarreled with her lover, the Marquis of Great Peru. Having heard that the narrator, Monsieur de C... (Corneille), is a sorcerer, she begs him to turn her into a zombie, so that she can terrorize the Marquis. He refuses, but when she offers sexual favors, he pretends to make her invisible, after which she goes on nocturnal rampages at the Marquis's house. After a certain amount of sex, betrayal, humiliation, and slapstick all around, our narrator ends up in prison again, this time accused of sorcery.

One of the peculiarities of this tawdry little story is that it marks the first recorded use of the word "zombie" (or, in this case, *zombi*). It had a more general meaning then than now, and was applied to a variety of ghosts and nocturnal terrors. Its only previous appearance in literature was a Zombi who led a slave revolt in the Brazil in the 1620s. It's not known if that was his name, or his title.

One of the other peculiarities of the book is that it appears to be somewhat true. Louÿs and Loviot combed through the colonial records for the "key" to its people and places.

The Marquis of Great Peru was

Charles Dupont, the son of Marguerite la Garrigue. The Countess of Cocagne could only be Félicité-Françoise-Antoinette de Lespinay. She had somewhat of a reputation: after bearing a child by one of her mother's slaves (which she then promptly strangled), she bore several more with one of the servants, Jean Roland, whom she eventually married. He, of course, is "Roland le Débonnaire." Research also turned up a Benjamin de Gennes, and a servant named La Forêt.

The story takes place on the island of Basse-Terre, mostly on the south, between the towns of Basse-Terre and Capesterre. Grand Pérou was a sugar plantation between the Capesterre and Pérou rivers. Marigot was on the right bank of the Pères river, Carbet on the right bank of the Carbet river. The Dos-d'Âne (Ass's Back) was a mountain, later renamed Gourbeyre, between Capesterre and Basse-Terre. Louÿs even found a pond named Zombi.

Whether accurate or not, Blessebois's tale presents a scathing view of colonial society. The self-styled Barons, Princes, and Marquis spend their days in orgies, drinking, gossip, superstition, and church. The Countess herself goes barefoot, lives in a hut, and serves her guests tadpoles. Labor is done by slaves and conscripts. It's worth mentioning that the word for conscript, *engagé*, also means someone who has signed a pact with the Devil. In the story, Jule is the conscript who works for the

Marquis, but Blessebois was one too.

The "historiette" is written in prose alternating with verse. The verses often serve as commentary; Blessebois uses them to express his pious hypocrisy, self-pity, justifications, and misogyny. It's quite a performance. The verses are a mixture of alexandrines and octosyllables, with an occasional decasyllabic line thrown in. I rendered them as blank iambic pentameter and tetrameter, which seemed to give the best results with a minimum of paraphrase. I could do nothing about all of the mixed metaphors, nor about the jaw-dropping nastiness of the "Portrait."

Although several commentators have said that the text contains many Creole words, I found few. There's *zombi*, of course, and *marigot*, which means swamp: the Barony of Marigot, I'm afraid, is rather pathetic. The "Foreign Prince" is from Les Irois, in Haiti; I translated "Irois" as "Haitian," to make things clearer. I kept the place names in French, except for Grand Pérou, which I give as Great Peru to keep the title all in English.

Guillaume Apollinaire wrote an introduction to an edition of Blessebois's works, which appeared in the *Bibliothèque des curieux* in 1921. The book contained *Le Zombi*, as well as *Le Rut* and *Lupanie*, the last of these probably not by Blessebois. Apollinaire based his introduction on Édouard Cléder's preface to the 1862 edition, apparently unaware of Loviot's later findings. Apollinaire included the introduction in his proposed collection of essays on libertine literature, *Les diables amoureux*, published posthumously in 1964.

I consulted the editions of *Le Zombi* from 1697, 1860, 1862, and 1921, all scanned and available online. I reprint here the list of characters added to the 1862 edition, since it may help. Let me also acknowledge Frédéric Lachèvre's 1927 biography, and his undated pamphlet *Une revendication de Pierre Louÿs: la clef du Zombi du Grand Pérou*. Eugène Revert's *La magie antillaise*, 1951; Sophie Houdard's *Les figures de l'auteur-escroc chez Paul-Alexis Blessebois, dit Pierre Corneille Blessebois (1646?-1697?)* (*Cahiers du Centre de recherche historique*

35, 2007); and Doris Garraway's *The Libertine Colony: Creolization in the Early French Caribbean*, 2005, were all truly helpful too. I'll let Blessebois have the last word, defending his character during a trial in 1672:

"Are you not that wicked boy who has debauched so many young women?"

"No, I am that young man who has been debauched by so many wicked women."

New York City
March, 2015

Preface

by Guillaume Apollinaire

The poet and novelist Pierre-Corneille Blessebois was born around 1646, not in Alençon, as some have said, but in Verneuil, or near there.

This singular writer, who called himself the "wandering poet," came from a good Protestant family. Destined for a military career, he went to Alençon, and, from that point on, his scandals and adventures filled a life whose details are still largely unknown. We know that he changed religion several times, and that, unscrupulous, but a "born lover," he seduced many women and cost them dearly. It was at Alençon that he met Mademoiselle Marthe de Sçay, who visited him in the prison where he had been sentenced for the crime of arson. After leaving prison, he continued his scandalous and amorous intrigues, and, after a duel, having abducted Mademoiselle de Sçay, who also bore the name of Marthe Le Hayer, was forced to take refuge in Holland. This woman from a good family, with whom he had been madly in love, became the object of a violent hatred that he expressed in his writings. It was in Holland that he published most of his works. It was there too that he enlisted in the navy. He later returned to France, and was in Paris in 1678. Around

1696, he found himself in Guadeloupe, where his position as a naval officer in the French galleys had taken him. In the Antilles, he became the hero of even more amorous adventures. He published *The Zombie of Great Peru,* and died sometime after 1697, the year in which we lose all trace of this aging "favorite of the beauties."

Cléder placed at the beginning of his edition of *The Zombie* (Paris, 1862) a scholarly preface, in which he assessed the talent and works of Blessebois:

"Let us now say a few words about the literary talent of Blessebois. His works can be divided into two distinct parts: the serious writings and the facetious writings. In the first part belong the tragedies

The Sighs of Sifroi, Eugénie, and *The Holy Queen*, and the comedy *The Crow*. We must place in the second his novels and stories, as well as his erotic and burlesque verse. One can see at a glance that burlesque verse best suited his talents; he felt more at ease, and the frankness of his manner led at times to flashes of wit and gaiety. His style, however, is almost always mannered, and suffers from a certain affectation by his use of new coinages and bizarre expressions, which express even more bizarre ideas. These serious flaws are more noticeable when he indulges his taste for licentious subjects, and tunes his lyre to the key of a tragic epic. There the shocking incongruity is felt most keenly, and you see him at every moment, in the midst

of the most interesting and dramat-
ic situations, fall into the tasteless
and the foolish, by the puerility of
certain details, the extravagance of
some ideas, and the burlesque style
in which he couches them. But perhaps we should not be too severe
with this writer, for, except for the
four following lines, which escaped
from him before he had read Boi-
leau's *Art of Poetry*, which the leg-
islator of Parnassus had just deliv-
ered to the public:

The cruelties of Fate, which wages endless war,
And forces me to bend beneath its heavy curse,
Has made of me a poet, who roams the Universe,
Attuned to all the sweets Parnassus has in store.

we find nowhere, in his writings,
that he took any pride in his com-

positions. His prose is no more pol-
ished than his verse, and the care-
less errors with which they abound,
and which might easily have been
corrected, are the clearest evidence
that he wrote only to fill his leisure
and to revenge himself upon the
women who had refused or be-
trayed him.

"He wanted to serve simultane-
ously Mars, Venus, and the Muses;
but we like to think, for both the
glory and pleasure of our hero, that
the first two divinities showed him
greater favor.

"We will not end this note, unfortunately quite incomplete, without
exonerating, up to a certain point,
of course, Corneille Blessebois of
the exaggerated reproaches direct-
ed against him by two celebrated

bibliophiles, Charles Nodier and Paul Lacroix.

"The first, in his *Miscellany Drawn from a Little Library* (p. 367), says, in reference to *The Zombie of Great Peru*: "Never has a pamphlet been more grossly suitable for the filthy orgies of a circle of idle and depraved men"; and the second, in a note to Volume II of his *Soleinne Catalogue* (Number 1465), levels this judgment: "This passage is not the only one that recalls the tone of some of the descriptions in the Marquis de Sade." This rigor and severity seem exaggerated, to say the least. Needless to say, we have no desire to become the apologist of Corneille Blessebois, or to proclaim his morals as exemplary, and his writings as paragons of taste and decency; but *The Zombie* remains far superior to the *Lusty Ladies* of Brantôme and the *Love Life of the Gauls* of Bussi-Rabutin, which Charles Nodier never thought to smite with his wrath, and which he sometimes even mentions with indulgence.

"As for the reproach addressed to him by M. Paul Lacroix, we find it at the very least also unjust. We have searched in vain through the works of Blessebois, even the most daring, and found nothing like the cynical tableaus and vile maxims which teem upon every page in most of the writings of the Marquis de Sade. Corneille Blessebois is a licentious poet, that is undeniable; but his writings are no freer than those found in the *Satyric Parnas-*

sus, the *Satyric Cabinet*, the *Cabinet of Bawdy Muses*, the *Satyric Broadsword*, the *Follies*, etc., and the author can be placed with his contemporaries Régnier, Sigogne, Maynard, Théophile, Berthelot, Motin, and others, who have distinguished themselves in this genre of poetry, and whose works, prized by the curious and scholarly, have never been the object of such rigorous censure.

"Charles Nodier himself, who often indulged in ill-considered condemnations and exaggerated praise, according to the nature of his impressions, granted this type of literature a large place in his own library, because he understood better than anyone that it offers, in addition to the merit of rarity, which is not always the least for some bibliophiles, a certain interest to anyone concerned, in a more or less direct manner, with the history of the human mind."

We must add to these lines, so full of sense, that one of the merits of Blessebois, or at least the one which brings him particularly to the interest of the literate, is that by writing *The Zombie of Great Peru* he gave France her first colonial novel. At that time, exoticism, and especially American exoticism, had supplied nothing to French literature, except travel memoirs and geographical collections.

With *The Zombie*, the islands appear in French literature with numerous words from the Creole vocabulary. And in this regard, *The*

Zombie is a linguistic monument worthy of closer study. To begin with, this little book, extremely rare, remained for many years all that French literature owed to exoticism. *The Zombie* marks an extremely important literary occasion, and anyone who would write the history of the colonial novel in France must not forget to mention the name of Pierre-Corneille Blessebois, a very unusual author, about whom we know very little, for we remain as uncertain about his place and date of birth as the place and time that he died.

Characters Who Appear in
THE ZOMBIE

The Marquis of Great Peru

The Marquis's mother

The Marquis's sister, the Baron of
Marigot's mother

Jule, the Marquis's conscript

The Marquis's chief bursar

The Viscount of Carbet, the Marquis's
brother

A Negro in the Viscount's service

The Baron of Marigot, nephew of the
Marquis of Great Peru and of the Viscount
of Carbet

The Baron's younger brother

The Baron's sisters

The Baron's niece

The Countess of Cocagne, mistress of the
Marquis of Great Peru

Roland le Débonnaire, the Countess's
husband

A Negro in the Countess's service
The Count of Bellemontre, the Countess's
brother-in-law
The Countess's farmer
The Chevalier of Capesterre
M. de C... (Corneille Blessebois,
author of "The Zombie")
His Highness of Les Irois, foreign prince
The great-nephew of His Highness of
Les Irois
Boüé, from Les Irois
Benjamin de Gennes
The Marquise of Saint-Georges
The servant La Forêt
M. de La Croix
La Sonde
M. Dufaux
Mademoiselle Dufaux
Cadot
Florimond
Nicolas Sergent

THE ZOMBIE
OF GREAT PERU

OR

THE COUNTESS OF
COCAGNE

Historiette

"As a jewel of gold in a swine's snout, so is a fair woman which is without discretion." These words of Solomon well suit the Countess of Cocagne. Everyone knows that she does not lack charms, for a Creole; but that her beauty is in no way embellished with chastity, constraint, or modesty. She has such a fierce hatred of virtue that she scorns any man with even a scrap of it. She is a sow adorned with the gold of her beauty, who finds pleasure only in the mire, and in the shamefulness of her conduct. She is always ready to prostitute her honor to her appetites, and the only ones who trust her are the instruments of her daily debauch.

If this young woman tried to hide her lust,
  Her efforts would be all in vain.
Her folly fixes to her foolish heart,
Her heart conveys it to her wretched soul,
Her soul then spreads it forth in raging floods,
From which she forges chains to bind her flesh.
  Her flesh submits, a loyal slave:
  A slave that is so brutal to
  The God whom it defies and scorns
  That it does evil, tricking Him.

I was alone in the house of the Marquis of Great Peru, one morning, when she paid a visit. Although she walked barefoot, like an Indian, her glory nevertheless shone through her disorder, and her pride seemed to have come only to insult my humility. She lay in a hammock, and told me that she had come to discuss a service that I could render her without harming anyone.

I suspect, I replied, that your discussion is hardly necessary for my salvation; nevertheless, you may propose, and if there be anything reasonable in your request, perhaps I can satisfy you.

> This scrupulous and cautious way
>   Of promising some future prize
> Provoked a laugh upon her rosy mouth,
> Where love held out a tantalizing hook.

—You are well aware, she said, that I have quarreled with the Marquis of Great Peru; but you may not know the cause, and I am certain that you will find it strange. Learn then that on the last night that he came to me, he was so drunk that he could scarcely put one foot before the other, once he had descended from his horse; and ill luck had it that he saw Boüé, the miserable Haitian who now works for the farmer of the Count of Bellemontre, my brother-in-law. At first, his jealousy mounted on stilts; he shouted more insults than he had drunk glasses of wine; he ran sword in hand after the boy to kill him; but God willed that he fell, and I carried him to my bed, where he slept for hours with as little sign of life as if deprived of it. After this first drunken stupor, he opened his eyes and hands, to cast them upon me, as I sat on a chair by the bed, thoroughly enraged by his recent insults. I proudly spurned his caresses, and refused to lie at his side. I reproached him in turn, and with such just and reasoned re-proaches, that he had the effrontery to strike me. This action, which I certainly had no reason to expect, provoked me to violent rage, and, losing no time in vain complaints, I gave him the same with a vigor which is not natural to one of my sex, and which gave him something to consider. Nevertheless, having recovered a bit from his surprise:

—You are quite bold, Countess, he told me, to dare to lay a hand upon a man!

—And you, Marquis, I replied, are you not a true scoundrel to en-joy my hospitality, to come to my bed seeking favors, and then to thank me with your fists? If you had not been as drunk as a pot of soup, would you not have sacrificed

Boüé to your cruel jealousy, and by that brave deed destroyed my honor? What liberties do you take in my home? Am I your wife? Do you dream of becoming my husband? And would you not have been otherwise engaged, if your vows and services had been accepted by that young lady to whom you recently offered them in such Spanish style? I swear to you that I will no longer be so easy, and that you will oblige me by not coming to poison my bedchamber with that stink of wine that you give off when you are here.

—You are right, Madam, he said as he left, and I promise you in the future more rest than you would like. You are not poorly counseled, but I doubt that those fine counsels will find you long willing to follow them.

The Marquis had a point, of course,
For if I recollect aright
The lusty woman told me that
She'd rather spend a year in the Abyss
Than lie one night alone in bed.

In fact, the Countess spoke those last pathetic words with such a heavy sigh, that I understood that she found the Count's boorishness easier to bear than his absence. Which is why, after considering her with scorn:

—It is God, I said, who gives a man a good woman; but I suspect that it was the spirit of mischief that gave you to the Marquis of Great Peru. A good woman builds and cares for her home, but you, who are senseless, not only destroy your own, but make your neighbor's totter on its foundation. You foolishly love a man who would be mad to love you; you are married, and want him to wed you; you offend him, and do not want him to be offended; he overlooks your faults, and you cannot suffer his; and finally, you chase him from your home, and do not want him to obey.

—No, she interrupted, and if you keep your word, you will see him back in my arms; you know the methods, I am sure, and I beg for your help.

And then her lovely eyes became
Two springs that overflowed with tears,
Which ran like rivers down her face;
I saw them flood the most resplendent flowers.
These faithful witnesses of her distress,
To tell the truth, affected me.
But I had many troubles of my own.
To comfort her, convinced I could not help,
My poor complexion turned so many shades,
It only spurred that scheming crocodile.

What is more, I firmly believed that she was only making sport of me, and had opened my mouth to protest, when she closed it with a credulity which opened the theater for the play to follow; which was, in essence, only a bagatelle, but which, nevertheless, others might denigrate as a tragedy, had I not drawn the truth from its well.

And so it was that from a spark
A mighty conflagration flamed.
If that comparison is none too new
At least it is a fitting one.

—You seem surprised, Monsieur de C..., resumed the Countess. Do you think that the Marquis has not told me what you can do?

—And what can I do, Madame?

—Anything you like, she continued; good and evil are equally in your power, and you can inflame both love and hate as easily as another man might light a torch.

—Apparently I am a sorcerer, I retorted.

—No, she insisted, but you are a magician; you keep the Devil at your command, and it is some of that art that I request to regain the Marquis's favor.

> My Countess, you have spoken well.
> I am the only of my kind,
> Because the Devil plays no part
> In any of my secret skills.
> For when a mistress I dismiss,
> I work my spells by other means,
> More binding, and of greater strength.
> And when upon the verdant ferns,
> Within the orchard or the wood,
> I taste a shepherdess's charms,
> I charm the shepherd boy away.

This pleasantry dried her tears more effectively than the most pious consolation that I could have offered; for, just as the slightest thing made her weep, the slightest thing could also make her laugh. But, so as not to leave her with an impression not to my advantage:

—You have a cunning mind, I told her, and your tongue has trouble restraining itself when you talk. I have a secret reason for doubting that the Marquis told such sinful tales; but, if you are telling the truth, I also have reason to fear that he may spread his nets to catch me; I will try to set things aright.

Although the fowler be the best,
I always can evade his cunning snares;
For all the graying Crows like me

Take inspiration from the fox.
It's difficult to trap a grizzled Crow.

This show of good humor encouraged her to redouble her impertinent pleas, and to promise me mountains of gold in the future, if I would only make her invisible, and help her in her plan to frighten the Marquis in his bed, scold him for his inconstancy, and threaten him with endless torment if he did not keep his promise to marry her, after doing all that he could to annul her first marriage.

Do not deceive yourself, Madame,
I told her in my gravest tones,
I swear by Heaven, and by Earth,
No God I know can lead a man to love
Except by your enchanting eyes.
So summon all their potent force,
For they will better serve your plan;

They are the rulers of this realm.

—Ah! You certainly take your time to decide, she answered; do you think, then, that we do not know that, when you served in the French galleys, you lived solely upon your commerce with the Black Angel? In any case, all who returned with you praised you so, that we believe no marvel beyond your powers. I ask only that you make me invisible for a single night; would you be so obdurate as to refuse a young woman whom you sometimes find pretty, and must I have the misfortune to be your only lover who reaps no benefit from your sublime knowledge? Ah! Monsieur de C..., do something for me, and...

I interrupted: that's enough,
Your sorry fate afflicts me so.
Perhaps some day we might improve your luck.
I shall consult my many books,
Each chaptered into many parts,
And if I have some sway in love's domain,
The Marquis of Peru will soon return.
But now it's time you leave; fly down the path,
The servant La Forêt returns.
And if that spy, whose unrelenting hate
Is ever fixed upon yourself,
Should see us chat together here like this,
He too will chat, and spread his slander far.
And as you know, the Marquis's jealousy
Is hot enough to kindle at a fly.
Although he's mad, he wants you without blame.
That's why the time has come to go.
Leave all to me, make your escape;
Not only am I wise, but politic,
And Heaven likes to parry all my blows.

The Countess of Cocagne obeyed, and I was pleased at having rid myself of her at so little cost. She had barely crossed the river, when the

Marquis of Great Peru returned from Marigot. He was no cheerier than any poor native, having lost the best of his Negroes. This misfortune had befallen him the previous evening, and it was to distract him from his melancholy that I told him about my conversation with his mistress, and her desire to play the Zombie, so that she might frighten him and make him consult his conscience. At first, he thought it would be good to call her to our rooms, and laugh at her gullibility; but upon reflection, he put off the party until his return from Grande-Terre, where he was to go the following day to cut wood for his watermill.

I don't know if his jealousy

Had made a great impression on his mind,
As minds of lovestruck men are often seized.
But he was in a reverie all day,
  And sighed in sorrow and distress.

Although I had taken precautions when I confided in the Marquis, the Foreign Prince, who kept an apartment and slaves at Great Peru, and had been spying on us from afar, suspected something. He gave me no rest until I told him all; and, since he loved nothing better than pleasure, he urged me to assign him whatever role I liked in the comedy.

  I readily accepted him,
And at my words his joy showed on his face.
  He proved a useful ally, too,
For he could play a villain fairly well.

Three days passed without the aspiring Zombie returning to her assault, and on the evening of the fourth, I happened to meet the Countess near the Marquis's sugar mill, where she had come to beg me to show her an example of my occult doctrine. We had been drinking freely; she noticed this, and adroitly profited from the situation. Seeing that I needed my ear pulled, but that my resistance was weak, she kissed me so tenderly and so touchingly that all of my pride dissipated, and I gave her every sign that she wanted of my cooperation.

What can a tender kiss not do
To touch a man's responsive heart?
This token spurs him on to hopeless tasks;
It makes him dare and venture all.

Not long after supper, His Haitian Highness and I retired to the upper room, where the Marquis's conscript lay trembling with fever. Old La Forêt remained below, and had locked the storeroom, and everyone was still awake, when the Countess of Cocagne entered through the back door, which I had carefully left open, and came up to our room disguised as a snow white Zombie, believing herself invisible. The Foreign Prince, as I said, had been told, but she knew nothing of this, and it was upon him that we had decided that she would enact her masterpiece. At first, she strode about the room; she furiously rattled the windows; she struck us one after the other, and did so many different and surprising things that old

La Forêt below was stricken with terror, and asked me several times what was wrong. We replied, the Foreign Prince and I, that we were being beaten, but could see nobody. The Marquis's conscript said the same, and he was not lying, for he hid in his bed, so effectively that it convinced the Zombie that he too wanted to be invisible. At last, the Countess of Cocagne, having in-flicted many little mischiefs on the Foreign Prince, turned him so deft-ly from his bed to the floor, that the building shook as if from a thun-derbolt, and we ran downstairs, the conscript and I, as fast as if the most terrifying death were after us. Old La Forêt took a long time to open the door; he was so alarmed that he mistook the kitchen door for that of the storehouse, and wanted to hide in the closet rather than light the lamp. Our cries summoned the Marquis's chief bursar, and when we could see what we were doing, we ran to help the Foreign Prince, who pretended to be struck dumb, and who imitated a swoon with such obvious affectation that he almost gave away the deception. None of us had the courage to return to bed; we sat up all night discussing the Zombie's affection for Great Peru, and old La Forêt swore to us that it had returned in thirty different ways since he had lived there.

In order to support his foolish thought,
    I said the demon was so foul,
It turned my soul to ice, and scared me so,
    That I saw two instead of one.
    Its hair was made from writhing snakes,

Its body was a harpy's, and
It carried in its godless claw
A vile chimera, spewing flames.

This success, which the simplest of men could have achieved as well as I, made me into the Phoenix of clever folk, in the Countess's mind. She rewarded my imaginary skill with infinite compliments, and with the sweetest caresses that I could imagine, all for a service of so little importance. I brought the Foreign Prince to her, so that she could see the man that she thought she had fooled. She made him repeat a hundred times the fear that he had felt, the way the Zombie had thrown him to the floor, and the vow that he had taken never to sleep in the upper room again. And her joy was so complete at having become invisible, and at holding the power to do so again through my agency, that one might think she had gone mad, or had drunk from the waters of that poetical fountain, which causes uncontrollable laughter in all those who quench their thirst there.

No creature is as weak as woman is,
 More frightful than the fires of Hell,
 And stormier than any sea.
Each holy virtue meets an iron heart,
And blackest crime will find a willing hand:
The Cruel Angel knots her blindfold tight.
 The silly beast will even place
 Herself in the most parlous spot,
 That's sure to bring about her end.

The Countess did all that she could to insinuate herself into my thoughts, and to learn to become invisible on her own whenever she pleased. I had only to suggest that I wanted something, for her to set everything in motion to get it; and this power that I had obtained, without any extraordinary deed on my part, continued in no little way to rekindle in her heart the passion for the Foreign Prince that had once enflamed her. He followed me like my shadow, and there was none more proper than he; he even responded with adequate grace to all of the parts that I had him play; but he was so transported with joy, to be once again in the saddle, that the part of him that was not very much turned Zombie, and often became invisible when asked to show some vigor. Nevertheless, the Countess had the discretion to complain to nobody but me, and I consoled her easily by giving her permission to return to frighten the guests at Great Peru. That night, the Foreign Prince was not there; but his great-nephew took his place in my room, and Monsieur de la Croix lay downstairs next to old La Forêt. Everyone was asleep, except me, when the Countess, infatuated with her supposed invisibility, came to prowl around the building, in a costume far better imagined than the first, and which was in truth somewhat terrifying. I went downstairs to meet her, and had no idea how to let her into old La Forêt's room, because he had locked all of the doors, when, spying a lamp through a half open window:

—Leave it all to me, she said, there is an entrance ready, and you will see that I can do more than I planned.

If you have ever seen a vicious wolf
Ferociously attack a flock of sheep
To sate his hunger on a newborn lamb,
    In such a way the Countess dove
Into the window like some supple fish,
    Which, when it senses danger near,
    Will break the water's crystal calm.

I retired quietly to my room, and was scarcely in my hammock, when I heard all of the furniture overturned below, all of the doors violently opened, and a hailstorm of blows visited upon old La Forêt and Monsieur de la Croix. The cries of the former could be heard as far as Marigot, and the latter was simply struck unconscious! The Countess believed herself so invisible, that she did not even douse the lamps, and walked between those good people's beds, with the same assurance as if her body's composition were as ethereal as it was material. Her rampage lasted for a half hour, and it was a miracle that she was not discovered, for all of the Marquis's Negroes, as well as the Marquis's bursar, ran to the aid of old La Forêt, entering just as she left, and by the same door.

That she could hide so well from all those eyes!
Without consulting oracles, I guessed
    Her faith could overcome all checks;
For she could lodge a boulder from its seat,
And work a wonder by herself alone.

There had been so little frivolity in

the Countess's actions, that old La
Forêt was seriously hurt on his hand
and left leg; and the good old man
was so confused in his hasty con-
clusions, that he sometimes blamed
me for the attack, and sometimes
the Marquis's bursar. He wept like
a little child, and fear had rooted itself so deeply into his heart, that he
lit a second lamp, and begged us to
sit awake with him.

I thought the poor old man would die.
He swore to us an oath that broke my heart.
A thousand times I cursed that woman's harsh
    And unforgiving spitefulness.

Word of mouth in Capesterre,
where it flies more swiftly than
gossip about a general in his army,
had published the news in Marigot

before sunrise, and everyone aired his opinion, according to the strength and prudence of his own imagination. Some were so perceptive as to declare that the Zombie of Great Peru could be none other than the Countess of Cocagne under my auspices, and concluded from our collusion that I could easily marry her, if Roland le Débonnaire were stupid enough to die. I wrote to the beauty about this, merely to sound the depths of her heart, and received such a passionate reply, that I understood that if I wanted to become a perfect idiot in every particular, I had only to offer my hand and to accept hers.

Although I'm ugly and quite old,
My proposition seemed to suit her well.

She saw it in its most propitious light,
    And was beholden to the Gods
    For something that was heaven-sent.
    No ugliness of any man
    Had ever turned her from her lust.
    For she is like a fisherman,
    Who prizes everything he hooks.

    O you who read this little work,
    If you should ever chance to meet
    This mother of my sorry sin,
    I'm sure that you would rue the loss
    If you should flee her cunning words.
    For she will find a hundred ways
    To quicken you to her desires.
    For she is like a poisoned spring:
    Beware that woman's appetites.
    It's safer to confront a bear
    Who's hunting for her stolen cubs.

We went to breakfast with her, the Foreign Prince and I. —Good morning, beautiful spirit, I said, as I greeted her.

—Be well, my master, she answered; use your servant according to your desires, and be assured of my very humble gratitude.

—Ah, my malicious one, I replied, once we were seated, I wanted to give you pleasure, but I did not want you to hurt anyone, and you were wrong to injure old La Forêt so cruelly; he was swimming in blood when we went to help him, and I feared the time had come for death to take him from his misery.

—You are mocking me, she answered, and that old dog would have been well served had I broken his head, as punishment for all the insults with which he blackened me the other day, in the presence of the Great Peru, who only laughed.

—That is all very well, Madame, I

added, but what offense had Monsieur de la Croix given you? He is an honest man, and you had no reason not to spare him. Fortunately, he was wrapped in bed, with the sides of his hammock together; if not for that, I could no longer number him among the living, and we would soon be in the hands of the magistrates. That is not good, Madame; you should moderate your fury, and not abuse your invisibility that way.

—Ah, how agreeably tickled I am with your account, the crazy woman cried, and how well avenged I am upon that old wolf, who recently called me a whore, and said he knew no hotter bitch on the Island. Would to God, she continued, that I had beaten so thoroughly all those who insulted me, and who have only to await their turns.

In Nature everything, I said,
　Has its appointed time and place,
　Variety is what She likes,
She brings it out in all that She creates.
　The gentle look beguiles the heart,
　The laurels suit the victor well,
　The hen will lay, the cock will crow,
　The bee makes honey in its hive,
　And I am good, and you are bad:
I hope for Heaven, you are bound for Hell.

This reflection caused her such a transport of delight, that we took our breakfast, the Foreign Prince and I, unable to persuade her to taste even a morsel of the things that she had served in such abundance. But the dessert that she gave us deserves mention.

This poor unhappy victim of
The sting of universal scorn
Surprised me as a lion might
Surprise a frightened little lamb.
The wantonness of her desire
Had so enhanced her loveliness
That my resistance could not hold,
And all my virtue gave me no support.
With all my wisdom flown away,
Voraciously I bit the lowland fruits.
And with the overwhelming spell
Of flattering and sugared words,
She won my soul, and so seduced my heart,
Which did not put up much defense.
If you enjoy a bit of fun,
The sly persuader said to me,
Then we can pass a pleasant hour,
And satisfy our hearts' desires.
And then, with an audacious look,
She touched me with a soft caress.
I found myself completely tamed
When she confessed her lassitude.
Preparing for our tender strife,
Beforehand she'd perfumed the bed
With orange buds and China blooms.
We crushed those scattered flowers so

That I was wounded by a thorn
Which gives me still a thousand pains.

We spent the rest of the morning in absolute joy, and in laying new plans to play the Zombie, and above all to frighten the Marquis's mother, who visibly opposed her happiness, and was the principal impediment to their marriage; for the Countess had spread the word of Roland's death, and shown publicly a false testimony that she had prepared, to use when all other difficulties were lifted. The Foreign Prince entered completely into our plans; I had them confess, one after the other, that they had known each other before, fully and at leisure. Nevertheless, we did not tell the Countess that he had been in my confidence the first time that she played the Zombie; on the contrary, I reassured her on this point, so as to prepare a dish to her taste, and to give the powerful Haitian something to do.

I'm certain that His Highness had
No more than half a heart for this.
By screwing with the Countess, though,
I knew that I had set the man
Upon the path of etiquette.
And I encouraged him in this,
Although he didn't like her very much.

She informed me that day that when her mother was still alive, she sometimes read a book of magic, which the good woman had carefully kept, and that she found it so much to her liking, that she could have become famed in the art, had she not been prevented; that the book contained a plethora of secrets about incredible wonders, but all put into practice. Above all, she mentioned a certain wax figure, which represented an enemy, and with which one could wreak invisible vengeance at will. She asked if I knew about it; I answered that I did, and for the moment she was satisfied.

But scarcely an hour after we had taken our leave of the Countess, the Baron of Marigot's little brother came into my room; he brought from her a block of wax the size of a fist. The child said that she requested me to make two images, one resembling an old woman of seventy years, the other a young man in his adolescence, and that I should not fail to deliver them before retiring, if I wanted her to be assured of my obedience. I saw directly the truth of the matter; one needed not be a sorcerer to solve such an obvious riddle. However, whether it was because it was not my profession to fashion dolls, or because I took slowly to the task, the sun had hidden from our sight by the time I had roughly sculpted an old woman, such as the Countess of Cocagne demanded, and it was that alone that I took to her.

Enchanting sinner, please accept, I said,
 This simulacrum of old age.
To grant your wishes, I would soften steel.
 But nothing's secret on this earth,
The truth will out, and I will be attacked
 And slandered as a sorcerer.

She contemplated it a thousand times, from head to foot, and finding the likeness better realized than she had perhaps expected, she kissed me so much, and with such fervor, that I had no doubt that I had done her a great service. She did not at first inform me what she planned to do with the figure; she contented herself with saying, as she gazed at it:

—Ah, Margot! I have you now, and I will cause you at least as much sorrow as you gave me in the past, if you do not move more quickly in the future.

The name Margot finally made her grotesque plan clear to me, but I made no show of it, so that I might have the pleasure of hearing it from her own mouth. —Your work is not done, my master, she said; you must perform an act of friendship, and prepare this image like the ones that I described to you. I am all yours; do you not want to be all mine as well, and follow my wishes, as I have sworn myself to yours? I will not deny that you have depicted the Marquis's mother admirably, and that I hope to thwart her if she continues to be troublesome; put then the finishing touches to your work, and make Margot susceptible to all of the ills that I would have her suffer, if that is what I need for my serenity.

—I am more obedient than you suppose, Madame, I answered, and the charm is already in it; but please, use it with discretion, and do not harm poor Margot as much as you can; you must have a bit of conscience in what you do, and it will be enough to make her languish a little, by sometimes holding her by the fire, or giving her a pinprick in the buttocks when she opposes your love for her son; for, if you are carried away by rage, and cast her in the fire, or go so far as to pierce her brain, the Marquis's mother would die in an instant, and what would become of our souls? You can also prevent her from making water, and deprive her of other necessities, as long as you like, by stopping up the natural conduits with a little plug of common wax. But once again, Madame, be discreet, and do not reduce me to the point of repenting my blind obedience.

—No, no, Monsieur de C..., she interrupted brusquely, have no fear, sleep soundly, and rest assured that

I lock my anger in such strong irons
that it cannot escape without my
leave. But, she added, I asked for
two images, and you brought only
one; think then to make the other,
and come tomorrow with the Foreign Prince, to eat the tadpoles that
I will have my Negroes catch.

She had no need to urge me so,
Already I was loath to leave her side.
So well she'd caught my heart with all her charms,
And so well lit the tinder of my love,
That though her house was just a filthy hole,
Where I could only enter on my knees
    To capture the distilling drop,
    I liked it better than Peru.

I had taken only ten steps away,
when she called me back to tell me
that she was brave enough to meet

the evil spirit who was the ordinary minister of my wishes and the secretary of my commands, and that I might give her that satisfaction. I confess that all of my composure could not prevent me from bursting into laughter at this extravagance; but my violent joy did not last, and I promised her seriously that I would let her smell the breath of the one that she had indicated. That did not even begin to satisfy her; nevertheless I repeated so many times that it was enough for a first attempt, and that creatures like that only let themselves be seen a little at a time by novices in the profession, that at last I took my leave without further promises.

I was surprised at her temerity;

Her soul revealed its sordidness in full
    Upon this new and strange request,
    Because, to tell the simple truth,
The very thought is such an evil one
That it can scarcely go unpunished long.
    The wildest panther will not set
    Upon her path with careless haste.
    The instinct that directs her steps
    Will clear the path in front of her;
    She has a sort of innate awe
    That makes her fear the lion's rage.
    But when a woman has no faith,
She yearns to stumble, and she craves the fall.
    She flies to ruin in delight,
    And flees whenever reason speaks.

I met the Foreign Prince on the other side of the river; I told him everything as it had happened; he was as astonished as I, and swore that she was capable of any evil, and that the Devil himself would be less bold than she in committing an extraordinary crime. The next day, we were persuaded of it by an occurrence which would make anyone wary. We went that evening to eat tadpoles, as invited, but before we sat down to dinner, I asked her to show me Margot, so that, I said, I might see by her condition the disposition of the original.

—Ah, in fact, she said, Margot is all broken; I have no idea who played with her, but she has not a single limb in place.

—Well, this is going nicely, I replied, and it only confirms my judgment that you are worthless, and leads me to believe the rumor that the Marquis's mother is very ill. Show me, show me Margot, so that I may visit her, and try to heal her injuries; I am sure to cure her, for twenty-four hours have not passed since the harm was done.

The Countess of Cocagne opened a little Caribbean chest which served as a casket for poor Margot's useless remains, and, having finally taken the doll into my hands, I found a shattered leg, an arm broken in three or four places, her eyes gouged out, and her head stabbed here and there eight times by a monstrous needle. I feigned extraordinary sorrow, as the Foreign Prince scolded the Countess suitably for her misdeed, and advised her to find some way to console me. She gave me more than a hundred kisses, one after another, after which I made Margot whole again with little trouble; but I did not think it right to return her, even though it was a vain and ridiculous thing, because she offended God just as much with this figure, as if it had been a living creature that could feel real pain, because of the ill will that she had shown.

But when a woman's born to practice vice,
Though you prevent her, soon or late she yields;
And if you can at times delay the crime,
   And even thwart the fatal plan,
   You only stir her malice up.

We sat at the table, and feasted on the Countess's tadpoles; and we were on the point of leaving, when she reminded me of the figure of the Marquis of Great Peru, and of the secretary of my commands, whose breath I had promised that she could smell.

  —As for the image of your servant, I told her, you are not yet ready for it; I know from experience that you proceed too hastily for me to place, under your power, the life of a person who is dear to me, and to whom I may be under some obligation; but here is a candle which holds the spirit who obeys me. I shall light it, and when he decides to have his breath smelt by the company, I shall be quit of my promise.

It was a piece of the wax that she had sent by the Baron of Marigot's little brother; it contained a long shaft from a turkey feather, which the Marquis's bursar had filled with gunpowder; one might have thought it a torch, and I had so calibrated the little devil, that it not only produced the effects I expected, but blew smoke into the Countess's nose without causing her offense, but in an admirable manner, which seemed to target her alone, and thoroughly surprised her. She then truly believed in me, and urged me to work miracles to which I was as blind as any mole, when the Marquis's conscript arrived, delivering this little speech on the part of his master:

—Madame, he said to her, Monsieur has returned from Grande-Terre, and he sends me to tell you not to forget to come to Great Peru tonight to play the Zombie again, and to treat his bursar as you treated his sugarer; he challenges you, you and all of those who interfere to give you such good advice.

We had not expected the Marquis so early, and his arrival surprised all of us; words failed us, and the conscript would have left without a re-ply, when, with an instructive glance at the Countess, I saw her conceive on the spot the reply that she had to give; and, since she is easily moved, and put great faith in my protection:

—Jule, she said to the Marquis's conscript, tell your master that he is not to give me orders, and that if the fancy takes me to go to Great Peru, it will not be upon his bursar that the Zombie will do his work, but upon himself, and he should not assume more courage than he has.

Although she dreaded his return,
She made believe that she was brave:
The partridge menacing the hawk.
A woman who is full of guile
Is like a fathomless crevasse
Whose depths are hidden from our sight,

Who weeps inside while seeming to be glad,
And laughs when she pretends to weep.

The conscript departed quietly, and we discussed matters with more prudence than we usually could summon. We had decided, the Foreign Prince and I, to go to the river in Goyave; the Countess of Cocagne had loaned me a horse, but it had no saddle; so we went to Great Peru to borrow one. I entered openly, and the Marquis, who was in bed downstairs, gave me every caress imaginable; but his jealousy did not tell me what it thought. He did not speak to the Prince, and His Haitian Highness said nothing to him either. After a few indifferent exchanges:

—I do not have the key to your room, he told me; my bursar put it in his pocket. You can call him, he is out among my slaves' huts.

—No, Marquis, I replied, I thank you; my plan is not to retire for the night; we are taking a ride, His Highness and I, and will mount our horses in a moment, if you would be so kind as to loan us a saddle.

> To ask the least of favors from
> A man whose jealousy you goad
> Is not the way to mollify his ire.
> It is exceedingly unjust.

As soon as I had made this request, his conscript, who had orders to spy on our activities, whispered in his ear that the Countess of Cocagne had loaned me one of the horses from the Islet, and that I had it tethered to one of the bagasse huts. He had no doubt that the beauty was in our party, and, brusquely rising from his bed:

—Jule, he cried, have my horse saddled, and a moment later he rode off to her house, where God knows how he treated her. We saw from the garden that when he passed the bagasse hut he took my horse and led it back to the Islet, and that obliged us to go ask the Baron of Marigot to borrow another, and a saddle, for the Foreign Prince, but he wanted nothing to do with the matter, so that His Highness returned to Great Peru, and I stayed the night at the Baron's house, at his insistence.

Barbaric fate, which wages war with me,
And bows me underneath its crushing laws,

Refuses me four inches of this earth,
    Not even land enough for me
To sleep, as foxes can, in my own den.

I firmly believe that God inspired that young man to shelter me, for we learned later that the Marquis had resolved to murder me that night at Great Peru; and the next morning, he arrived in a towering rage to attack me at his sister's house. But the Baron, although his nephew, firmly turned him away, with such honor and hospitality that I am eternally indebted to him. He is so incapable of the rumors that have circulated against him, that one can say, on the contrary, that he is the soul of honesty, and has so much modesty and good sense, that all who know him could never refuse him their esteem without declaring themselves open enemies of virtue. And a great proof of it is the obstacle that he placed before his Uncle's attempt to murder me.

Why must one trample underfoot
A man because he has no home?
The highest angels of the Lord
Were once no more than we are now.
Do power and authority
Confer integrity to man?
How very wrong the error is!
But I am done, my fate is sealed,
And if I live, or if I die,
I live and die in poverty.

It was Sunday, and after the Baron's family had consoled me for the harm that he had intended, and we had taken our breakfast, we attended mass; and from church we returned to Marigot, where we enjoyed an orgy that reigned two hours longer than did the sun. Most of the principal inhabitants were in the party, and whoever wanted to mix black with white, satisfied himself without trouble in the warehouse of Benjamin de Gennes, where a little Ethiopian Cupid lifted the barrier for all those who chose to enter the fray. But although there was great freedom, there was no other offense, to my knowledge, and we parted more honorably than is usual when we quit Marigot after a day of debauchery.

For Bacchus never ruled with more restraint,
And never did wine kindle fewer fights,
Or poison less the pleasure of the meal.
And Venus never showed herself more kind,
Or kept the holy Father more in check.

Everybody had already mounted their horses, and we were leaving as well, the Foreign Prince and I, with la Sonde, whom we held under the arms, and who had asked us to stay at his place, when the Viscount of Carbet, having remembered that I no longer had access to Great Peru, returned at a gallop, and forced me to take the croup of his horse. I say that he forced me, because His Haitian Highness and la Sonde wanted me to keep them company, and I was quite ready for some rest.

In an instant, we had rejoined the Baron of Marigot, and since wine was our guide, and drunkards are insatiable, we paid a call on the Chevalier of Capesterre. There we found Monsieur de la Croix, and after having all drunk to one another's health, with the wine from the two bottles that the uncle and nephew had brought, we rode off to do the same with Monsieur Dufaux; but only the Viscount of Carbet and I arrived, the Baron of Marigot having slipped away under cover of darkness. Mademoiselle Dufaux opened the door in her nightshirt, and told us that her husband was not there; but the Viscount soon found him, and we managed to empty our bottle, and bade them good night.

The beauty we had roused from sleep
Reluctantly arose from bed;
But our departure helped console
Her sorrow that we'd ever come.

I thought that after having prowled around so, the Viscount would probably take me to sleep with Carbet, or his nephew, but when I complained that he was going the wrong way, and that I could barely hang onto his horse:

—My brother left this morning for Grande-Terre, he told me, and asked me not to return to Carbet, until I had seen how things were at Great Peru. We will go there, and on our return I will take you to my sister.

—Fine, fine, I replied, it's the Foreign Prince's pretty little Negress that takes you there, not your brother's business; but it makes no difference, go wherever you please, provided that you ride your horse less roughly; however, I promised the Countess of Cocagne yesterday that I would see her today, whatever the time.

—If my brother catches you, answered the Viscount, I warn you, he will caponize you; be careful.

—He will not catch me tonight, I replied, because he is in Grande-Terre. Please do not leave without me; I will only stay a moment.

The Viscount gave his horse to his Negro, who had not left him; he went to Great Peru, and I went to the Countess of Cocagne.

Just as a dolphin never sleeps,
And never stops to rest both night and day,
    Or as a quiet peaceful lake
    Is agitated by the storm,
    Like them, a man will never rest;
    He's always ready day and night
    To carry out some wicked deed.
    His ear's alert to every sin;
    He always finds it when it calls,

Wherever it may be concealed.

—You come quite late, she said to me; where did you leave the Foreign Prince?

—I sent him to play the Zombie for the Marquise of Saint-Georges, I replied, and tomorrow you will hear that he wrought so much destruction in your service, that you will love him half again as much as before.

—Then you made him invisible? she asked.

—Yes, Madame, I continued, and after you have made me happy, I will also go to terrify the Marquis's mother, as you have often asked me to do.

My wishes were agreeably received, after which she led me back to the river, where she planned to wash herself.

The desire overtook me to see her totally naked, and I waited for her to remove her clothes and her shirt to join her; but no sooner had that beautiful mass of flesh struck my sight, and no sooner had my eyes received the snowy splendor of her lovely body, than my heart was kindled with a new flame, and I returned to my vomit with a passion that I had not felt before. She joyfully admired the magnitude of my delight, and, without lying, I rattled off a thousand compliments on hers, which it would be impossible for me to repeat, even if prudence did not forbid it.

This unrepentant prostitute,
With all her dangerous delights,
Has cost the strongest men their lives;

The Island is obsessed with her.
The Ugly Angel uses her,
Much like a net, to capture us,
And damn our weak and helpless souls.
Her craftiness would soften steel;
Her home, ablaze with raging flames,
Lies on the road that leads to Hell.

I had already risen to leave, when she asked me to make her invisible.

—I cannot do it tonight, I told her; wait until tomorrow.

—No, she replied, let us not wait until tomorrow, I beg of you.

—Because you want to know everything, I replied, know, Madame, that the method I used to make the Foreign Prince invisible, and which I will use for myself, has nothing in common with the way that you played the Zombie at Great Peru. It is as spirits that we will go tonight, to flutter here and there, while our bodies remain in the willows, or under some rock far from the road.

—Well, then, she interrupted, no matter, take me with you; I am already naked, and my body will be safe here.

—You are stubborn, Madame, I said; but in fact I desire all that you desire, and will arrange it so that the surrounding Zombies, who are my little cousins, will come to carry you away; but I must warn you to lie still on your back, and to keep your eyes and mouth closed, for if you happen to move, or to see or say anything, your life would be over. You may hear voices that will try to make you speak; be very wary of them; the spirits are clever, and will seduce you if you believe them, and I would be very sorry if any harm came to you. I will prepare those things that are needed for my flight. Adieu, Madame; if you wish to come with me, follow all of these instructions carefully. If not, take a bath and return to your hut; that will be simpler.

When I look deep within myself,
Then I can see the evil fruit.
For I am like a child at night
Who sees a pale and spectral form;
I am a hundred times more stirred
And tossed than saplings in a wood
When Boreas breathes out his worst.
And yet, alas! One moment more,
The weathercock has spun again,
And I am dreaming further schemes.

I was in such haste to distance myself from that foolish woman, and to laugh at her simplicity at my leisure, that I fell face first into the river. I recognized the Count of Bellemontre's farmer, in the Marquis's bagasse hut; he was at least as drunk as I was. I told him about my shipwreck, and warned him to be careful; I then regained the croup of the Viscount of Carbet's horse, and he took me to his nephew. I gave them a faithful account of all that had passed between the Countess of Cocagne and myself, but they thought that I was spinning tales, and refused to believe me. The Baron of Marigot gave me his hammock, and took a bed that was in their room, despite his uncle, who wanted to take him to Carbet. The Baron's mother also had the kindness to get up and give me some linen, for I was a pitiful sight, and chilled to the bone. I slept like a log, and had been in bed for over three hours, I think, when the Viscount of Carbet returned to ask his nephew to go with him. They vanished in the blink of an eye, and the Baron's mother came down to my room, and had a long chat with me. She complained that her brother was debauching her son, and was saddened that they went off chasing women at such an ungodly hour, and almost naked. She would have talked all night, but I kept dozing off in my answers, and her charity would not permit her to deprive me of the rest that I so badly needed. The sun had already arisen while I still lay in bed, and I was slowly getting dressed, when the Viscount of Carbet's Negro came to the Baron's mother to fetch her son's clothes, and a horse to bring him back. A moment later, I went to the Chevalier of Capesterre, where I found the Foreign Prince, who was purchasing a gross of gloves, and who gave me a pair. We drank some brandy, and I asked His Haitian Highness to accompany me back to the Baron's mother, to show the young ladies how to make gold and silver fringe. He told me on the way that he had already visited the Countess of Cocagne, and that she said that I had tricked her; that instead of making her fly in spirit form to frighten the people at Marigot, as I had promised, I had summoned Zombies to swarm around her, who had played a thousand malicious pranks on her, and that she no longer wanted to love me. He had, however, calmed her anger, and he had no doubt that I could make peace with her again.

> I am as deaf as any post,
> And pay no heed to all that woman's noise;
> She's lost all honor, I can say,
> And nothing turns her stomach now,
> And what occurred was just a harmless joke.

We found ourselves in good company at the house of the Baron's mother. Benjamin de Gennes, who was there, and who missed not a word of the news circulating about the new guest, told me that there was a great deal of gossip about the violence committed against the Countess the night before, and that I was the one principally accused.

—Ah! replied the Baron's mother,

this time I can testify to the injustice against M. de C...; he slept here, I chatted with him for much of the night, and we can both swear, if necessary, that I did not leave his hammock after half past ten, at the latest, when I gave him a change of linen.

—Truth is strong, I said to Benjamin de Gennes, and lies are weak; they dissipate like a cloud; and I shall summon the Countess of Cocagne, so that you may hear from her that she has no complaint with me, or at any rate none like those of which the scandalmongers accuse me.

I felt myself so innocent
Of everything that had transpired,
That, in all conscience, I could care
No more about it than for broken glass.

Aha, I murmured to myself,
The lion always stalks his prey
With all the glory of a king.
He makes us frightened for ourselves
Much more than for the sheep he kills;
And every man, because he fears
Some greater danger, lets him be.
But when a fox comes from the wood
To prowl about some little town,
He cannot snatch a single hen
Without endangering his life.

In less than a quarter hour after I had sent a Negro to her, hers came to whisper in my ear that she was at the gate, and asked to speak with me. I went to meet her, and began by reprimanding her. I have never seen her look more insolent than she did then.

—I am the one who has a quarrel with you, she told me, and you are playing my part. You have not badly tricked me, Monsieur de C...! Your devilish little cousins did a thousand rude things to me: they pinched my ass, bit the tip of my nose, and pulled out half the hair from that part that you love so. Never have little monkeys taken so much pleasure in plucking a poor chicken, than they took in pulling out hair after hair. They did all they could to make me speak, and to open my eyes, which I had covered with my handkerchief. They even imitated the voices of the Viscount of Carbet and the Baron of Marigot, and put a rosary on my arm to make me think that they were not evil spirits, but I was too smart to believe their deceptions. They took all sorts of shapes, and I thought at times that I had a hundred rats on my face, on my body, and at the tips of my fingers and toes, where, as you can see, they boldly bit me.

—Is that all they did, Madame?

—Eh! she replied, what else would rats do but bite?

—But, I continued, the spirits who assumed the voices of the Viscount of Carbet and the Baron of Marigot, did they put their profane hands on that place that I love the best?

—Have I not told you, she said, that they put a rosary on my arm, and that they plucked me, pinched my ass, and even whipped me with branches; but the one who spoke like the Baron of Marigot did not want the other to whip me, and said:

—For shame, my uncle, why mistreat this poor woman so? Take

her back to her hut; day is coming, and everyone will see her here.

—Very well, Madame, I said, he was the only one you should believe; he was a good spirit who took pity on your weakness, and to whom you should wish no ill. They did not tie you up and garrote you, as gossip has it, for you yourself confess that they could not even overcome your resolution enough to move you from a place where you could be exposed to the sight and mockery of everyone.

—You had ordered me not to, you bad boy, she replied, and I was even more certain that they were evil spirits who were playing so many tricks, because all around me it smelt so strongly of brimstone, that I was faint of heart at every moment.

—It could smell of nothing but brimstone, I replied, laughing, because Zombies never fly, to frighten people, without carrying torches made of it; and you are fortunate, Madame, not to have seen them, for the sight of them is fatal, and no human can withstand their somber light.

> She could not find a single word
> To answer to my worthless speech,
> For human nature is so base,
> It credits evil more than good.

We were at that point in our conversation, when Benjamin de Gennes, the Foreign Prince, the Viscount of Cabet, the Baron of Marigot, his little brother, his mother, his sisters, and his niece came out, and invited the Countess of Cocagne into the house. They did not have to twist her arm, and once we were seated, the conversation turned to the Zombies of Great Peru, and to the adventures of the previous night. She admitted that she had become a spirit, but denied that she had been mistreated, and vomited a thousand curses against those who circulated such lies.

Although a figure of disgrace,
She still could haughtily maintain
That wisdom was her sister, and
Judiciousness her only friend,
Just as a murderer at times
Will drape himself in monkish robes,
So he might better play the part.
And just as I have often read,
That when a wolf skulks to the kill
It wears the shearling of a sheep.

I think that we never laughed as much at the Baron's house, as we laughed that morning; each of us had his reasons to laugh, and if I had not firmly decided to leave for Basse-Terre, I imagine that the curious Countess would have once again begged me to turn her invisible, for she no longer remembered the pains that she had suffered, and the thorns at the beginning of our intrigue only made her yearn for the roses that she foresaw at its end; but my horse was waiting, and I could no longer delay my voyage, without running the risk of having to make it on foot, which would have been too tiring. The Countess of Cocagne, who could not consent to my departure, seeing at last that I was determined to go, asked me with tears in her eyes to wait for an hour, so that she could borrow a horse and accompany me properly, but the Marquis's bursar took the horse from between her legs, so that I set out alone, but only after the Viscount of Carnet and the Baron of Marigot had sworn with terrible oaths that, not only had they not dipped their bread into the Countess's milk pot, but that it had never even occurred to them; and I decided for several reasons that they were innocent. Someone more perceptive than I might have judged differently; be that as it may, I wash my hands of it.

No earthly thing eludes a prudent man,
For, in the crystal surface of a stream,
   He sees his portrait shining forth
   When he goes there to wash his face.
   And so a wise and prudent man

Can always easily discern
From any creature's outward sign
Whatever lies within its breast.
And speculation never mars
His marvelous divining skill.

As I traveled, I reflected a thousand times upon the adventures of the Zombie of Great Peru, and on the gullibility of the Countess of Cocagne; and my soul took on as many different colors as a chameleon. My sin frightened me when I considered Heaven, but I found it so beautiful when I looked to Earth, that I even convinced myself that men owed me a great deal of obligation, and that they would be ungrateful should they refuse me praise for my amorous victory, and laurels for my brow. So it is that sin blindfolds us, and deprives us of our reason; for, after all, whatever mortal man might do,

No wisdom will he ever find
In anything that counters God.
His reasoning is always vain and weak;
He sees his Hell on every side.
For he's been filled with darkness since
That early day the cruel serpent spread
Within his fragile simple heart
The poisoned honey of its vicious words;
And now, in everything he does,
His passions keep control of him;
For man is blind when he is born;
He's still a child; a hundred times
A day he falls into the lions' den.

That is how I applied a brush to the picture of my sins, and how I sighed in sorrow at my weakness for pursuing the delights of the flesh. But those virtuous impulses were only fleeting, and, from this confession of my errors, I fell at once into the insolence of trying to excuse them by citing famous examples from antiquity.

I, like a sinner, murmured to myself,
Did Adam, David, Samson, Solomon,
And Lot not bite into the fatal fruit?
I've heard it said a hundred times in church.
And if it's true that honest souls like theirs
    Have burned so for a woman's love,
    Alas, how can unlucky I
    Resist the flames that they could not?
    Am I a wiser man than they?
So cease, my heart, and do not sorrow so.
Not everyone is virtuous enough
    To parry all the blows of flesh.
The unleashed demons in the airy plains
Have subtly made me fall to lassitude;
    But I did not, like some sly fox,
    Surprise the chicken unaware.
    In all the pleasure that we took,
    No violence was ever used;
For, as it happened, she seduced the cock.

The cock, so full of kindness and good will,
    Just acquiesced to her assault.
    And if my predecessors took
    Their burins and engraved their names
    Upon the lady's pearly flesh,
I cannot now remember who they were.
    No sooner had she grown her breasts
    Than she'd begun a merry dance,
    A passepied from Brittany,
    To piping from a flageolet,
    Beneath the arbors of Cocagne,
    Valet and master at her side.

These fine thoughts, for which Heaven rightfully punished me, kept me company until I came to Three Rivers. I dismounted at Cadot's place, and that fine lad forgot none of his natural civility in his charming reception. We dined together, and with as much tranquility, and as much detachment from the worries of life, as Felix IV, after his papacy, in the Chateau of Ripaille. I entertained him with the story of the Zombie of Great Peru, and the foolishness of the Countess of Cocagne.

—I find nothing particularly criminal in any of it, he told me, and you are not to blame for the errors that the Devil inspires in those who seek him. Nevertheless, I do feel sorry for you, and the poor state of your current fortune makes me fear that it will be used as a pretext to declare you a criminal, and that malicious rumors, which spare nobody, may poison the innocence of your will, and blame you for the conduct of the public. I will be candid, he continued, it is said that you are a sorcerer, and that there is nothing amazing that you cannot do; gossip kills, and when people see a drowning dog, nobody goes to its aid.

—You are right, I replied, and far from being charitable to the unfortunate animal,

Each man will go, a stone in hand,
To aggravate the cruel show
And add to its unhappy lot.
And so, my dear Cadot, when man is poor,
His fellows vie to cast a stone
To send him sooner to his death.
If weakness makes a pauper fall,
It's said he had an epileptic fit.
No matter what a poor man does, he's just
A creature that the rich abuse,
In vain he may go calmly and in peace,
All men disdain him; he's despised by all.
The only thing that's prized is wealth.
And if a rich man has a fit,
The world will say that he was simply tired.
A wondrous metal then is gold,
And so contagious is the stuff,
That it is found around the world;
It is a pestilential wind,
Which some rebellious angel blows.

And gold inspires more bended knees
Than all the blood shed by our Lamb
Who suffered such a bitter death.
The fault's so great, the weakness is so strong,
They set the burden on the feeblest ox,
When they adored the Golden Calf.
Each gossip poisons the defense
Of any man who's destitute;
His lack of money will suffice
To make him one that all suspect.
He finds he has a foe in every man,
And though he may have done no wrong,
He's sacrificed by lying words.
And yet an evil fiend who earns God's wrath
Is like a bird that flies away
And nobody can apprehend.

—I am judged, I continued, by the color of my feathers, and am thought to be subtilized, because I sometimes dress an ode as an epistle, and because I know how to add a little azure and coral to the eyes and mouth of Phyllis and Sylvie; in short, I offend because, thank God, I am not exactly like other men, who are jealous of my conquests, and envy me because I know naturally how to evoke pity in a woman's heart, and can find Venus under the sign of the Virgin.

We were chatting in this way, Cadot and I, when sleep, which shows no more mercy than evil gossip, but whose wounds are more agreeable and beneficial, carried us in its arms until the break of day, when I mounted my horse to continue my voyage. I was so weak, and so sick at heart, that I had to dismount at every moment to rest; I was only running, so to speak, by wheels and springs, and yet, only two hours after sunrise I reached the Dos-d'Âne: that was a great effort for me in the state that I was in; but it is also true that I was exhausted, and that my courage failed when I considered the steepness of the mountain.

A hundred times I fully cursed Dos-d'Âne,
Although it could not hear a word I said.
Ah, cruel mountain, why could you not be
As easy to descend and sweet to mount
    As was the Countess of Cocagne!

At last, I had stopped to rest so many times that I fell unconscious, into a deep swoon. I was beginning to come to my senses, when I saw beside me Florimond and Nicolas Sergent, who rescued me with great charity, and revived me with brandy. I gave them my thanks as well as I could, and Florimond asked, gazing at me in pity:

—And where are you going, poor man? Are you so tired of life that you willingly take the road to death? Turn back, he continued, and if nothing can prevent you from wanting to die, and your hour has come at last, at least return to die in the arms of the Countess of Cocagne, and do not wait for the throne that is being prepared for you in Basse-Terre, by order of the court, to be completed.

—It is no jest, Nicolas Sergent added, and it is proclaimed that you have done such prodigious and criminal things, that I suspect that you will be condemned before you are brought to trial.

—To tell the truth, I answered seriously,

I find myself amazed at what you say;

But I'm not worried for my age,
For Heaven sets a limit, I am sure,
   On cruelties from wicked men.
It's true I screwed the Countess, I admit,
Now even little children know I did.
   I blame my weakness for the fact.
But even elephants can fall in love,
And frankly, and I hope I don't offend,
Have I not done what all the Island has?

—It is true, answered Florimond, that the Countess of Cocagne is the public breastplate, and that nobody grows bored at her door; but make no mistake, Monsieur de C..., it is not for biting the fruit that you are threatened with death; all of the magical powers bestowed upon you by the Little God of Hearts are coming to light, and you will not die an innocent man if all that is said is true.

To make your sins seem greater still,
They are portrayed in varied ways.
One man has made a solemn vow
The Countess takes on many forms by day;
    At dusk he saw her as a bull
    Who broke the water's crystal sheen
    To go to your savanna, then
    When she was some few steps away,
    Transformed herself into an ass.
The ass then spoke to him in human tones.
    But since his heart was gripped with fear,
    So that he almost swooned away,
    This human donkey took no heed
    Of what the magic ass declared;
    And yet he managed to recall
    The animal had asked him twice,
    Where are you going, brother mine?
That was the tangled tale the witness told:
    This scoundrel with a viper's heart
    Who spoke against his sister so.

    Another, also full of lies,
And maybe even more so than the first,
    Said one day, on a pigeon hunt,
    As he approached the beauty's house,
    He spied one in an elder tree

Which looked so lovely to him, that
He shot it, and it fell to earth.
But when he ran to pick it up,
It changed into a woman, who at once
Embraced him to demand a kiss.

One said he saw her as a sow,
With fifteen piglets at her side,
Upon the Marquis's land, where people pass
When they go to his sugar mill;
And in the verdant pasture there,
The merry sow and all her little pigs
Were dancing on their hinder hooves,
And in the center stood a rat-haired goat,
Who chanted in the common tongue
The orders for the Sabbat dance.

Another witness claims he saw
This evil spirit, late one night,
Go feeding something to the mill,
Which set it turning like a storm.
At last, when she grew tired of this,
He saw her flare up like a fire
Consuming old and rotten planks.
And as she flew away, she cried,
Today is Sunday, so I must

Dress up in all my Sunday best.

To add to all this foolishness,
It's said that all of Hell swarmed up
To screw the Countess, one by one,
Beneath the cliff, by dark of night.
And that you called those demons forth,
For you know all their names and all their ranks,
To offer them this sacrifice;
And that, that night you tried a thousand times
To transfer from your neophyte
Her welcome into your own flesh.

—If all that were true, I interrupted, I would be the cleverest man in the world, and could have spared you the trouble of rescuing me. I would have been in Basse-Terre long ago; and the Dos- d'Âne, over which I floated, would not have fatigued me so. But there is nothing supernatural in my exploits: there is only imprudence and indiscretion, and I do not fear my accusers.

A man who could become incensed
That I enjoyed myself too much
Should know that God created me,
And loves the creature that He made;
And if some day that man is bored
With his tranquility and peace,
He too may check his magic book;
But if at last my body's hanged,
Kind sirs, will it be very strange
To see a Crow up in the air?

I finished this speech, which made them laugh, then thanked them again, took my leave, and finally arrived in Basse-Terre, where I was eagerly expected, so that I could be housed in the filthiest and deepest dungeon in the fort.

END

A PORTRAIT OF THE COUNTESS OF COCAGNE
IN IRREGULAR VERSE

Her figure would be fine indeed
    If it were not so lean in front,
Which somewhat spoils it; she is game for love
Both day and night: beside her, or on top.

    If one believes the spiteful talk,
She doesn't have much hair upon her head.
But those who make that claim are not the best;
And it was not from there I saw her most.
    But elsewhere she has quite a crop,
    For she is often watered there
    With liquors of the sweetest kind.
My pen is just as truthful as it's bold.

Her brow, where lust and laziness are set,
    Is rather laudable, in fact.
But one will never see a blush of shame
    Nor any precious wisdom there.

    Her eyes are very like a pig's;
    They are by far the smallest here.
    No doubt they look the way they do
Because the life she leads is much the same.

    Her nose would be all right, I guess,
    If it could only catch the scent
    Of any scrap of decency.
On seeing it, one gives it little thought.
    But later, it can give the facts
About the depth to which her soul has sunk.

    The colors blooming on her cheeks
    Are reminiscent of the spring;
    But they are also wheels to break
    The many sinners of our time.

I scorn her breast, I find it badly made;
It is not firm, its swelling is too soft.
    It often drips a bit of milk,
Which is a household good that has its use.

And that must be the reason the Marquis
    Can use her like a dairy cow.
    Her arm's as white as it is plump;
    It is a thing of loveliness.
    And any heart would skip a beat
When such a peerless beauty comes in sight.

    The Countess is not unaware
    Of this perfection of her charms;
She has no doubt that it is unsurpassed.
The greedy woman wants that everything
Approaching her be made as well as that.

    Her hand is no less finely formed:
One thinks, on touching it, one handles silk.
    If something doesn't go her way
You'll see her fury billow up like smoke.
    The Countess then will raise that hand
    At morning, evening, afternoon,
Or any time of day the fuse is lit.

    And if her soul were half as white
    As her seductive pearly flesh,
    She'd be an angel; but instead
The Devil cannot sin as much as she.

Her feet two Creoles are, and both,
To tell the truth, are quite robust,
But also always caked with dirt.
At my most generous, I'd say
I would not give two pennies for the pair.

To all of this, I'll simply add
That for her pleasure, she has quite a bed.
And if I don't describe her mouth,
Dear reader, then she hasn't one.

ABOUT THE TRANSLATOR

DOUG SKINNER has contributed articles and cartoons to *Black Scat Review, Oulipo Pornobongo, The Fortean Times, Strange Attractor Journal, Fate, Weirdo, The Anomalist, Crimewave USA, Nickelodeon, Zuzu, Cabinet,* and other fine publications. His book of picture stories, *The Unknown Adjective and Other Stories*, was published by Black Scat Books in 2014.

His translations include *Three Dreams* (Giovanni Battista Nazari, Magnum Opus Hermetic Source-works, 2002), *Considerations on the Death and Burial of Tristan Tzara* (Isidore Isou, Black Scat, 2012), *How I Became an Idiot* (Alphonse Allais, Black Scat, 2013), *Captain Cap: His Adventures, His Ideas, His Drinks* (Alphonse Allais, Black Scat, 2013), *Merde à la Belle Époque* (various, Black Scat, 2013), and *Selected Plays* (Alphonse Allais, Black Scat, 2014).

He has written music for several dance companies, including ODC-San Francisco and Margaret Jenkins; his scores for actor/clown Bill Irwin include *The Regard of Flight, The Courtroom, The Regard Evening,* and *The Harlequin Studies.*

He lives in Manhattan, venturing from his garret occasionally to teach music lessons and to perform his music in discerning clubs and cabarets.

Sublime Works in Translation
Published by Black Scat Books

"... one of the great masterpieces of humorous literature."

—*nooSFere Littérature*

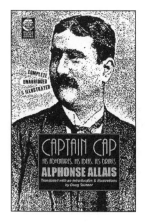

"...apart from being long-awaited, *Captain Cap* also comes at a timely moment because its ironies are particularly apposite today as we witness global intellectual colonization." —*Leonardo Reviews*

Translated and with an introduction, notes, and illustrations by Doug Skinner, this is the complete, unabridged text of the original 1902 French classic by the peerless humorist, Alphonse Allais. This deluxe edition also features eight uncollected "Captain Cap" stories, plus a "Cappendix" of rare historical pictures. Over 360 pages of absurdist mirth and howls of laughter.

"Allais comes across as a very modern writer, and his work as an experimental enterprise which is exemplary in many ways... it is also quite possible to invoke such writers as Queneau, Calvino, and Borges." —Jean-Marie Defays

This collection of Allais's rare theatrical texts includes original translations—never before published in English—of ten monologues, three one-act plays, and twelve shorter dialogues, skits and burlesques drawn from his columns in such publications as *Le Chat Noir* and *L'Hydropathe*. This delightful compilation by Doug Skinner (with fascinating notes on the texts) is proto-Dada at its most delicious.

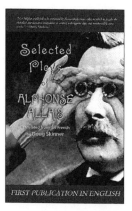

"No Oulipian could fail to be enchanted by his essentially ironic tales, in which he juggles the rhetorical and narrative components of writing with rigorous logic and inexhaustibly zany results."
— Harry Mathews

> *"No Oulipian could fail to be enchanted by his essentially ironic tales..."*
>
> —Harry Mathews

The Squadron's Umbrella collects 39 of Alphonse Allais's funniest stories—many originally published in the legendary paper *Le Chat Noir*, written for the Bohemians of Montmartre. Included are such classic pranks on the reader as "The Templars" (in which the plot becomes secondary to remembering the hero's name) and "Like the Others" (in which a lover's attempts to emulate his rivals lead to fatal but inevitable results). These tales have amused and inspired generations, and now English readers can enjoy the master absurdist at his best. As the author promises, this book contains no umbrella and the subject of squadrons is "not even broached."

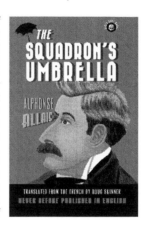

 Visit BlackScatBooks.com

More **BLACK SCAT BOOKS**

29436942R00087

Made in the USA
Middletown, DE
21 December 2018